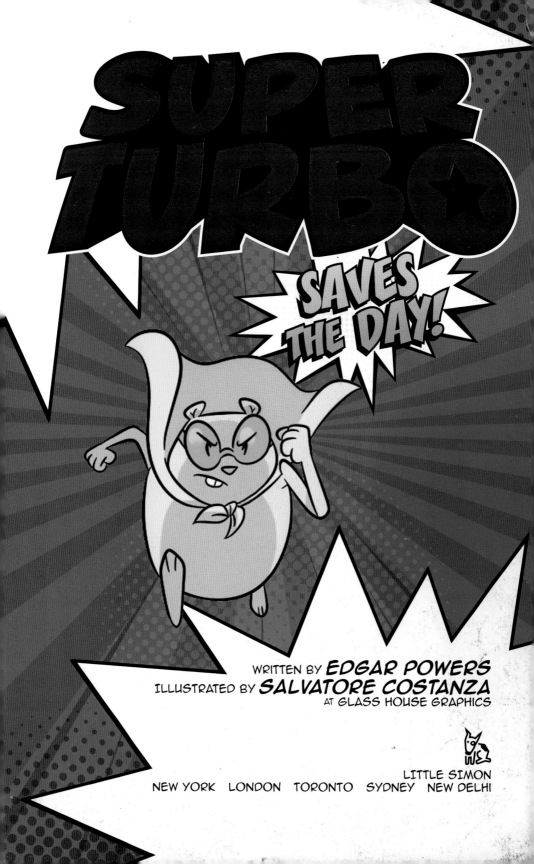

WRITTEN BY **EDGAR POWERS**
ILLUSTRATED BY **SALVATORE COSTANZA**
AT GLASS HOUSE GRAPHICS

LITTLE SIMON
NEW YORK   LONDON   TORONTO   SYDNEY   NEW DELHI

LITTLE SIMON
AN IMPRINT OF SIMON & SCHUSTER CHILDREN'S PUBLISHING DIVISION
1230 AVENUE OF THE AMERICAS, NEW YORK, NEW YORK 10020
FIRST LITTLE SIMON EDITION FEBRUARY 2021 * COPYRIGHT © 2021 BY SIMON & SCHUSTER, INC. ALL RIGHTS RESERVED, INCLUDING THE RIGHT OF REPRODUCTION IN WHOLE OR IN PART IN ANY FORM. LITTLE SIMON IS A REGISTERED TRADEMARK OF SIMON & SCHUSTER, INC., AND ASSOCIATED COLOPHON IS A TRADEMARK OF SIMON & SCHUSTER, INC. FOR INFORMATION ABOUT SPECIAL DISCOUNTS FOR BULK PURCHASES, PLEASE CONTACT SIMON & SCHUSTER SPECIAL SALES AT 1-866-506-1949 OR BUSINESS@SIMONANDSCHUSTER.COM. THE SIMON & SCHUSTER SPEAKERS BUREAU CAN BRING AUTHORS TO YOUR LIVE EVENT. FOR MORE INFORMATION OR TO BOOK AN EVENT CONTACT THE SIMON & SCHUSTER SPEAKERS BUREAU AT 1-866-248-3049 OR VISIT OUR WEBSITE AT WWW.SIMONSPEAKERS.COM. DESIGNED BY NICHOLAS SCIACCA * ART SERVICES BY GLASS HOUSE GRAPHICS * ART AND COLOR BY SALVATORE COSTANZA LETTERING BY GIOVANI SPARADO/GRAFIMATED CARTOON * SUPERVISION BY SALVATORE DI MARCO/GRAFIMATED CARTOON * MANUFACTURED IN CHINA 1120 SCP * 2 4 6 8 10 9 7 5 3 1 * LIBRARY OF CONGRESS CATALOGING-IN-PUBLICATION DATA NAMES: POWERS, EDGAR J., AUTHOR. | GLASS HOUSE GRAPHICS, ILLUSTRATOR. TITLE: SUPER TURBO SAVES THE DAY! / BY EDGAR POWERS ; ILLUSTRATED BY GLASS HOUSE GRAPHICS. DESCRIPTION: FIRST LITTLE SIMON EDITION. | NEW YORK : LITTLE SIMON, 2021. | SERIES: SUPER TURBO, THE GRAPHIC NOVEL ; BOOK 1 | AUDIENCE: AGES 5-9 | AUDIENCE: GRADES 2-3 | SUMMARY: SUPER TURBO LEARNS HE IS NOT THE ONLY SUPERHERO PET AT SUNNYVIEW ELEMENTARY. IDENTIFIERS: LCCN 2020024872 (PRINT) | LCCN 2020024873 (EBOOK) | ISBN 9781534474468 (PAPERBACK) | ISBN 9781534474475 (HARDCOVER) | ISBN 9781534474482 (EBOOK) SUBJECTS: LCSH: GRAPHIC NOVELS. | CYAC: GRAPHIC NOVELS. | SUPERHEROES—FICTION. | HAMSTERS—FICTION. | PETS—FICTION. | ELEMENTARY SCHOOLS—FICTION. | SCHOOLS—FICTION. CLASSIFICATION: LCC PZ7.7.P7 ST 2021 (PRINT) | LCC PZ7.7.P7 (EBOOK) | DDC 741.5/973—DC23 LC RECORD AVAILABLE AT HTTPS://LCCN.LOC.GOV/2020024872 LC EBOOK RECORD AVAILABLE AT HTTPS://LCCN.LOC.GOV/2020024873

CONTENTS

IT MIGHT LOOK LIKE A TYPICAL SCHOOL, BUT IT'S NOT. INSIDE THESE WALLS THERE IS A *BIG SECRET!*

BUT MORE ON THAT LATER. FIRST, THIS IS *TURBO!* HE IS A HAMSTER.

THIS IS TURBO'S *CAGE.*

I PREFER TO CALL IT MY *"PALACE."* CAGE JUST SOUNDS... *WRONG.*

THIS IS THE CLASSROOM WHERE TURBO'S *"PALACE"* IS. MRS. BEASLEY'S SECOND-GRADE CLASS.

AS YOU CAN SEE, TURBO IS THE CLASSROOM PET OF CLASSROOM C.

TURBO
Official Classroom Pet
CLASSROOM C

THAT'S *"OFFICIAL"* CLASSROOM PET. MAYBE I CAN TELL THE *STORY?*

TURBO
Official Classroom P
CLASSROOM

BEING AN *OFFICIAL* CLASSROOM PET COMES WITH *RESPONSIBILITIES.* I AM EXPECTED TO...

...GET *PLENTY* OF EXERCISE...

HUFF! PUFF!

...EAT PELLETS...

CRUNCH! MUNCH!

...AND DRINK *PLENTY* OF WATER! GOTTA STAY HYDRATED!

GLUG!

GLUG!

RUSTLE
RUSTLE

YOU HEARD IT THAT TIME, RIGHT? IT'S COMING FROM THE *CUBBIES.*

AS THE *OFFICIAL PET* OF CLASSROOM C, I MUST INVESTIGATE!

IT IS MY *DUTY!*

THERE MIGHT BE *DANGER.* I SHOULD BE PREPARED!

TURBO SILENTLY EXITED HIS *"PALACE"* AND MADE HIS WAY ACROSS CLASSROOM C TO THE SOURCE OF THE MYSTERY NOISE.

HE WAS SNEAKY, SO YOU MIGHT NOT BE ABLE TO SEE HIM. SO HERE'S SOME HELP.

THERE HE IS.

SEE HIM?

MAYBE?

CHAPTER 2

TURBO BRAVELY CREPT TOWARD THE *HORRIBLE MONSTER*. ONE GOOD YANK AND THE MONSTER WOULD HAVE TO SHOW HIMSELF...

HEY! CAREFUL!

I'M A *GECKO.* MY TAIL CAN BREAK OFF EASILY!

I'M *LEO*, FROM *CLASSROOM A.* WHO ARE YOU?

ANOTHER CLASSROOM PET? TURBO DIDN'T *EXPECT* THAT!

IN HIS CONFUSION, TURBO ACCIDENTALLY REVEALED HIS NAME!

WITHOUT A WORD, TURBO AND LEO DARTED ACROSS THE CLASSROOM FLOOR. THEY WERE *SUPER SNEAKY*, SO HERE'S SOME HELP TO SEE THEM.

HERE.

THERE.

PRETTY SURE THIS IS *TURBO.*

DEFINITELY TURBO.

POSSIBLY TURBO? OR A DUST *BUNNY.*

WATCH OUT!

WHO WAS THAT *MYSTERIOUS* FIGURE PEERING DOWN FROM ABOVE?

CHAPTER 3

ANOTHER CLASSROOM *PET?*
TURBO WASN'T EXPECTING THAT!

LOOKS LIKE
THE INVESTIGATION IS
OVER, SO I CAN TAKE
IT FROM HERE.

BUT THAT'S NOT MY REAL *SUPERPOWER!*

SUPERPOWER? YOU HAVE SUPERPOWERS?

HA-HA! SUCH A *KIDDER!* ALWAYS JOKING, THIS ONE!

I WASN'T JOKING! LEO, YOU KNOW THAT—

OKAY...

...I AM NOT JUST LEO. I'M THE *GREAT GECKO!*

AND I'M NOT JUST ANGELINA. I'M *WONDER PIG!*

YOU! GUYS! ARE! *SUPERHEROES?!*

CHAPTER 4

YES! THERE ARE **NOT** JUST OTHER CLASSROOM PETS!

THERE ARE OTHER PET **SUPER-HEROES!**

C'MON, I'LL SHOW YOU THE **WAY!**

THAT WONDER PIG SURE IS **STRONG!**

SUPERSTRONG!

HI, CLEVER!

MEET OUR NEW FRIEND, *SUPER TURBO!*

HE'S THE PET *PROTECTOR* OF CLASSROOM C!

ANOTHER SUPERHERO, HUH? THIS SOUNDS LIKE A JOB FOR...

WAKE UP, WARREN!

PROFESSOR TURTLE IS NEEDED!

YOO-HOO, WARREN! TIME TO WAKE UP!

INSTEAD, TURBO AND THE OTHERS WAITED FOR WARREN TO MOVE THROUGH THE DUCT TO THEIR NEXT LOCATION.

YOU *GOT THIS,* WARREN! ALMOST THERE!

OKAY, WE MADE IT! TIME FOR OUR LAST *STOP!*

IS THERE TIME FOR A *NAP?* THAT WAS EXHAUSTING!

NOPE.

HOW ABOUT A *SNACK?* I'M GETTING HUNGRY.

NOPE.

TURBO WONDERED WHERE THEY WERE GOING NEXT.

CAFETERIA

WHERE ARE WE GOING NOW? ANOTHER CLASSROOM? THE CAFETERIA?

NOPE.

THE *PRINCIPAL'S OFFICE!*

CHAPTER 5

TURBO HAD NEVER BEEN TO THE PRINCIPAL'S OFFICE...

...BUT HE KNEW *A THING OR TWO* ABOUT IT.

I ACTUALLY WASN'T WORRIED THAT IT WAS TERRIFYING, BUT NOW I AM!

SO, UM, WHO LIVES HERE?

YOU'LL SEE!

IT WAS **DARK** IN THE PRINCIPAL'S OFFICE.

TURBO SQUINTED AND SAW A **CAGE** WITH METAL BARS, SIMILAR TO **HIS** CAGE.

WE DON'T SAY "CAGE." WE SAY "**PALACE**," REMEMBER?

SUDDENLY THE *LIGHTS* WENT ON! THE CAGE... *ER, PALACE...* DID LOOK SIMILAR TO TURBO'S. EXCEPT THIS ONE CONTAINED...

...A *BUNNY!*

HI! DID YOU COME TO SPRING ME FROM HERE?

WE SURE DID, *FRANK!*

OR SHOULD WE SAY...*BOSS BUNNY!*

OH, SO YOU'RE HERE ON *SUPERHERO BUSINESS*, THEN? LET ME GET MY...

AND WITH THAT, TURBO'S NEW FRIENDS SPRANG INTO *ACTION*.

EVERYONE WAS HELPING...EXCEPT FOR TURBO.

HE JUST *WATCHED*.

WOW! THAT WAS *REALLY* IMPRESSIVE!

HELLO? WHO'S THERE? IS THAT YOU, *CLEVER?*

NELL? IT'S SO GOOD TO SEE YOU!

I THOUGHT YOU GOT *FLUSHED!*

NOPE! THEY JUST *MOVED* ME OUT TO THE HALLWAY FOR SOME REASON.

SUPER TURBO, THIS IS NELL! SHE USED TO BE IN CLASSROOM D WITH ME!

CAN YOU GET ME OUT OF HERE? THE HALLWAY IS *SO* BORING!

WE CAN FILL MY TURBOMOBILE WITH *WATER*, AND NELL CAN COME WITH *US!*

THAT IDEA IS...*CRAZY!*

WHAT ABOUT THE AIR HOLES? WON'T THE WATER *LEAK OUT?*

I THOUGHT OF THAT TOO. WE'LL USE *CHEWING GUM* TO PLUG THE HOLES!

CHOMP! CHOMP!

IT'S WORKING!

MAYBE WE CAN USE THAT *BOTTLE CAP* TO TRANSFER THE WATER!

CHAPTER 6

WE'RE READY TO *FIGHT* EVIL!

WHAT *EVIL?*

GOOD QUESTION! SO, UM...WHERE DO WE FIND EVIL?

WELL, I'M HUNGRY!

GREAT IDEA! MAYBE EVIL WILL BE IN THE CAFETERIA? PLUS, I'M HUNGRY TOO!

BOSS BUNNY, I THINK YOU'RE JUST *HUNGRY.*

WE *ALL* ARE!

TO THE *PANTRY!*

UM, TURBO? AREN'T YOU HUNGRY?

I AM HUNGRY! IT'S JUST... *BOSS BUNNY* SEEMED SO SURE HE SMELLED EVIL.

OH WELL. TIME FOR A SNACK! YOU CAN *NARRATE* WHILE I EAT IF YOU WANT TO!

LOOKS LIKE OUR SUPERHEROES ARE GOING IN FOR AN **ACTION-PACKED** SNACK ATTACK!

AS TURBO MUNCHED ON HIS *BAGEL*, HE NOTICED THAT BOSS BUNNY STILL SEEMED *DISTRACTED*.

TURBO SENSED SOMETHING WAS *WRONG*. WAS EVIL AFOOT? HE LOOKED LEFT...

HE LOOKED *RIGHT*...

AND THEN HE *SPOTTED IT!*

WHISKERFACE **THE RAT!**

I SEE THE PAMPERED CLASSROOM **PETS** OF SUNNYVIEW ELEMENTARY HAVE DISCOVERED MY **SECRET LAIR!**

WHY AREN'T YOU *SCARED?* I SAID, I'M GOING TO MAKE YOU MY *PRISONERS!*

WHY AREN'T WE *SCARED?* MAYBE BECAUSE THERE ARE *SEVEN* OF US...

AND JUST *ONE* OF YOU!

I'M NOT SURE WHAT'S HAPPENING RIGHT NOW, BUT I NEED TO BE ON *ALERT!*

NARRATOR, YOU TAKE OVER FOR A WHILE.

THROUGH A HOLE IN THE WALL, A STREAM OF HAIRY, BIG-EARED MICE CAME POURING INTO THE PANTRY.

WE ARE NOT *MICE!* WE ARE *RATS!*

I THINK YOU ARE CONFUSED ABOUT WHAT A RAT IS.

I MEAN, HAVE YOU EVER *SEEN* A RAT?

YEAH, YOUR RAT PACK IS MORE OF A *MOUSE MOB...*

ENOUGH!

RAT PACK! *TAKE THEM!*

OH NO! IT'S AN *ACTION-PACKED RAT PACK ATTACK!* THE SUPERHERO CLASSROOM PETS NEEDED A PLAN, *FAST!*

NOT REALLY HELPING.

I HAVE AN *IDEA!*

HOW MANY RAT PACKERS ARE THERE?

I'M GONNA NEED MORE GRAPES!

IN THE MIDDLE OF ALL THIS *CHAOS*, SUPER TURBO SAW HIS OPENING!

DON'T GIVE IT AWAY!

AN *EPIC* BATTLE ENSUED...

...WHICH SUPER TURBO *SOMEHOW* WON!

DON'T YOU MEAN, "WHICH SUPER TURBO, *OF COURSE*, WON"?

WHAT SUPER TURBO DIDN'T KNOW WAS THAT DURING HIS EPIC BATTLE WITH **WHISKERFACE**, THE TIDE HAD TURNED AGAINST THE **CLASSROOM PETS**.

INSIDE THE TURBOMOBILE, FANTASTIC FISH WAS LOOKING A **LITTLE SEASICK.**

MAKE THAT *A LOT SEASICK!*

AND THAT WAS JUST THE BEGINNING OF THE **MAYHEM...**

IT GETS *WORSE?*

THE GREAT GECKO ALMOST *GOT AWAY*...

DON'T BREAK MY *TAIL!* IT WILL GROW BACK AGAIN, BUT STILL...

EVEN WONDER PIG AND THE GREEN WINGER WERE BASICALLY *DOWN* FOR THE COUNT.

WHICH MEANT...

WHAT? WHAT DOES IT MEAN?

IT MEANS THERE WAS JUST ONE CLASSROOM PET *STILL STANDING.*

LET'S TRY THAT *AGAIN.*

IT MEANS THERE WAS JUST ONE CLASSROOM PET STILL STANDING... *SUPER TURBO!*

CHAPTER 9

WITH *CHAOS* ALL AROUND HIM, SUPER TURBO REALIZED THE *RAT PACK* WAS DISTRACTED. WHICH MEANT NOW WAS A GOOD TIME TO MAKE *HIS MOVE.*

THAT IS, IF HE HAS A MOVE *PLANNED*...

OH, I HAVE A MOVE PLANNED...

I JUST THOUGHT OF IT, BUT STILL...

IS THAT *FLYING*, THOUGH? OR JUST REALLY GOOD *JUMPING?*

CALL IT JUMPING, OR FLYING...BUT SUPER TURBO *SOARED* THROUGH THE *AIR!*

WHO CALLED IT JUMPING? THAT WAS DEFINITELY *FLYING!*

HE MADE IT!
MAYBE...?

SUPER TURBO TOOK A DEEP *BREATH*...

...AND WITH ALL THE *HAMSTER SPEED* HE COULD MUSTER, HE *RAN*...

...AND FLUNG HIMSELF THROUGH THE AIR.

HE MADE IT! BUT NOW WHAT?

YOU'LL SEE— OR HEAR— IN JUST A MOMENT!

THE FIRE ALARM WAS LOUD, ESPECIALLY TO THE EVIL RATS OF THE RAT PACK, WITH THEIR GIANT *MOUSE EARS*!

KLANGALANGALANGALANGALANG!

THEY HAVE MOUSE EARS BECAUSE THEY ARE *MICE*!

THE *NOISE* WAS TOO MUCH AND THE RAT PACK *RETREATED*.

SEEING HE WAS BEING DESERTED, WHISKERFACE BEGAN TO *SCREAM* AND *YELL.*

BUT IT WAS TOO *LOUD* TO HEAR WHAT HE WAS SAYING.

MAYBE HE'S *ADMITTING* THAT HE'S REALLY A MOUSE!

REALIZING HE WAS *DEFEATED,* WHISKERFACE RETREATED TOO.

WE'LL NEVER KNOW EXACTLY WHAT HE SAID, BUT SUPER TURBO IS PRETTY SURE IT WAS SOMETHING LIKE...

THIS ISN'T *OVER,* SUPER TURBO! *I'LL GET YOU!*

CHAPTER 10

Classroom C

LATER THAT DAY, THE NEW FRIENDS GATHERED IN CLASSROOM C TO TALK ABOUT THEIR ADVENTURE.

THAT WAS SOME *QUICK THINKING* WITH THE FIRE ALARM, TURBO!

BUT HOW DID YOU KNOW IT WOULD *WORK?*

FRANK, YOU **SNIFFED** OUT THAT EVIL BEFORE ANY OF US!

GOOD THING WE HAVE YOUR SUPER-SMELLING BUNNY NOSE!

WHAT CAN I SAY? THE **NOSE** KNOWS!

SUNNYVIEW IS IN GOOD HANDS, THANKS TO **ALL** OF US!

HMMMM...

WHAT IF THERE'S OTHER *EVIL* OUT THERE BESIDES WHISKERFACE?

LEO IS *RIGHT!* WE ALWAYS HAVE TO BE ON THE LOOKOUT!

FROM NOW ON, THIS SCHOOL IS UNDER THE *PROTECTION* OF...

UM, ANGELINA? LEO? YOU GUYS ARE *IN*, RIGHT?

OF COURSE!

YOU KNOW IT!

HE PUT HIS SUPER TURBO GEAR BACK IN ITS SECRET HIDING SPOT...

I'M COUNTING ON YOU TO KEEP IT *SECRET!*

...AND LOOKED *AROUND* AT HIS HAMSTER WHEEL, HIS HAMSTER PELLETS, AND HIS WATER BOTTLE.

TOMORROW, SCHOOL WOULD BE BACK IN SESSION.

FOR ALL THE STUDENTS AND TEACHERS, IT WOULD BE NO DIFFERENT FROM ANY OTHER DAY. BUT WE KNOW IT WILL *NEVER* BE THE SAME.

BECAUSE STARTING TOMORROW, SUNNYVIEW ELEMENTARY WAS UNDER THE PROTECTION OF...

CAN'T GET ENOUGH OF THE
SUPERPET SUPERHERO LEAGUE?
CHECK OUT THEIR NEXT
ADVENTURE...

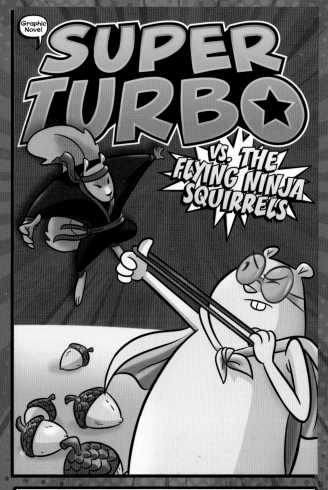

TURN THE PAGE FOR A SNEAK PEEK...

THE SUPERPET SUPERHERO LEAGUE HAD A TOP SECRET WAY OF *COMMUNICATING*.

IT INVOLVED *TAPPING* ON THE WALLS OF THE VENT AS AN ALERT TO THE OTHER PETS.

ONE TAP MEANT: "ALL IS WELL."

TAP

TWO TAPS MEANT: "I'M HUNGRY."

TAP TAP

AND *THREE TAPS* MEANT...

TAP TAP TAP